You Can Find the Class Pet, Pout-Pout Fish!

Deborah Diesen

Pictures by Isidre Monés, based on illustrations created by Dan Hanna for the *New York Times*–bestselling Pout-Pout Fish books

Farrar Straus Giroux
New York

Farrar Straus Giroux Books for Young Readers
An imprint of Macmillan Publishing Group, LLC
120 Broadway, New York, NY 10271 • mackids.com

Text copyright © 2023 by Deborah Diesen
Pictures copyright © 2023 by Farrar Straus Giroux Books for Young Readers
All rights reserved
Color separations by Embassy Graphics
Printed in China by RR Donnelley Asia Printing Solutions Ltd.,
Dongguan City, Guangdong Province
Designed by Gene Vosough and Aram Kim
First edition, 2023

ISBN: 978-0-374-39104-1 (hardcover)
1 3 5 7 9 10 8 6 4 2

ISBN: 978-0-374-39103-4 (paperback)
1 3 5 7 9 10 8 6 4 2

Library of Congress Control Number: 2022949540

Our books may be purchased in bulk for promotional, educational, or business use.
Please contact your local bookseller or the Macmillan Corporate and Premium Sales Department
at (800) 221-7945 ext. 5442 or by email at MacmillanSpecialMarkets@macmillan.com.

Mr. Fish was about to pout.

The class had a pet.

The pet was not in his home.

The pet was lost!

"How do we find him?" asked another fish.

The class made a plan.

"We will look for him!"

They looked in the room.
No pet.

They looked in the hall.
No pet.

They looked in the library.
No pet!

"Stay calm," said Mr. Fish.
"We will find him. I know it."

But he did not know how.

He looked up.
He looked down.
He looked all around.

Then he looked on his desk.

"I see him!"

The pet was found!

The pet is not lost.
The pet is in his home.

Now the class is happy.

So is the pet.

"No pout about it!"
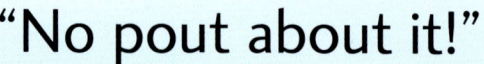